DETROIT LIONS

BY BRIAN HOWELL

Published by The Child's World®
1980 Lookout Drive • Mankato, MN 56003-1705
800-599-READ • www.childsworld.com

Acknowledgments
The Child's World®: Mary Berendes, Publishing Director
Red Line Editorial: Editorial direction
The Design Lab: Design
Amnet: Production

Design Element: Dean Bertoncelj/Shutterstock Images
Photographs ©: Paul Sancya/AP Images, cover; MRQ/
Icon Sportswire, 5; Tim Shaffer/AP Images, 7; Paul
Spinelli/NFL Photos/AP Images, 9; Scott Boehm/AP
Images, 11, 14–15; Susan Montgomery/Shutterstock
Images, 13; NFL Photos/AP Images, 17; Carlos Osorio/
AP Images, 19; Scott Grau/Icon Sportswire, 21; Cliff
Welch/Icon Sportswire/AP Images, 23; Scott W. Grau/
Icon Sportswire, 25; Steven King/Icon Sportswire, 27;
Greg Trott/AP Images, 29

ISBN 9781634070089
LCCN 2014959713

Printed in the United States of America
Mankato, MN
May, 2016
PA02315

ABOUT THE AUTHOR

Brian Howell is a freelance writer based in Denver, Colorado. He has been a sports journalist for nearly 20 years and has written dozens of books about sports and two about American history. A native of Colorado, he lives with his wife and four children in his home state.

TABLE OF CONTENTS

GO, LIONS!

The Detroit Lions have been around since 1934. They have one of the best football traditions. They are one of only two teams that host a game every Thanksgiving. It is a tradition that started in the Lions' first season in Detroit. The team was great in the 1950s. But the Lions have had many tough years since. Let's meet the Lions.

Quarterback Matthew Stafford runs with the ball during a Thanksgiving game against the Green Bay Packers on November 24, 2011.

WHO ARE THE LIONS?

The Detroit Lions play in the National Football **League** (NFL). They are one of the 32 teams in the NFL. The NFL includes the American Football Conference (AFC) and the National Football Conference (NFC). The winner of the NFC plays the winner of the AFC in the **Super Bowl**. The Lions play in the North Division of the NFC. Through 2014, they still had not reached the Super Bowl. Only three other current teams have not played in the big game.

Running back Barry Sanders's speed and sharp cuts made it hard for defenders to tackle him.

WHERE THEY CAME FROM

The Detroit Lions started as a team in Portsmouth, Ohio. The team was called the Spartans. They joined the NFL in 1930. The Spartans played for four seasons. They had a winning record three times. George A. Richards bought the team in 1934. He moved it to Detroit and renamed it the Lions. He also changed the jersey colors to blue and silver. The Lions won the NFL Championship in 1935. They won three more titles from 1952 to 1957. But through 2014, the Lions had only won one other playoff game.

Wide receiver Herman Moore made four straight Pro Bowls from 1994 to 1997.

WHO THEY PLAY

The Detroit Lions play 16 games each season. With so few games, each one is important. Every year, the Lions play two games against each of the other three teams in their division. Those teams are the Chicago Bears, Green Bay Packers, and Minnesota Vikings. The Lions also play six other teams from the NFC and four from the AFC. The Lions have been **rivals** with the Bears and Packers for more than 80 years. The Lions franchise has played Chicago at least once a season since 1930.

The Lions and Bears have had many memorable battles on the gridiron over the years.

WHERE THEY PLAY

The Lions played most of their games at Tiger Stadium from 1938 to 1974. It was also called Briggs Stadium. They shared it with the Detroit Tigers baseball team. Then the Lions played at the Pontiac Silverdome from 1975 to 2001. Now they call Ford Field home. Ford Field is an indoor stadium. That allows the Lions to play comfortably even during the freezing Michigan winters. The stadium holds 65,000 football fans. Ford Field is a busy place. It hosts dozens of other sporting events and concerts each year.

Ford Field has hosted wrestling events and concerts in addition to Lions home games.

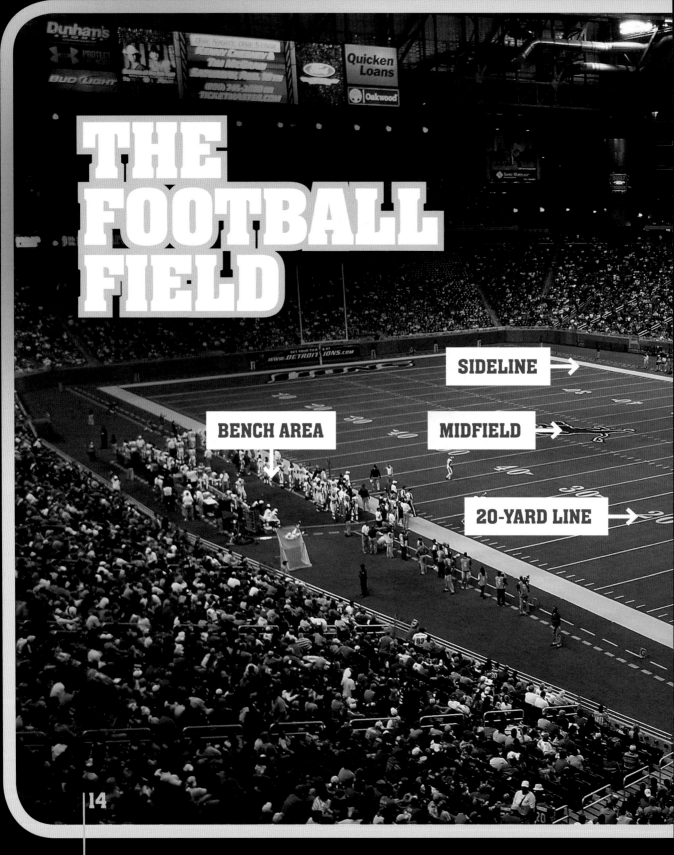

THE FOOTBALL FIELD

SIDELINE →

BENCH AREA

MIDFIELD →

20-YARD LINE →

14

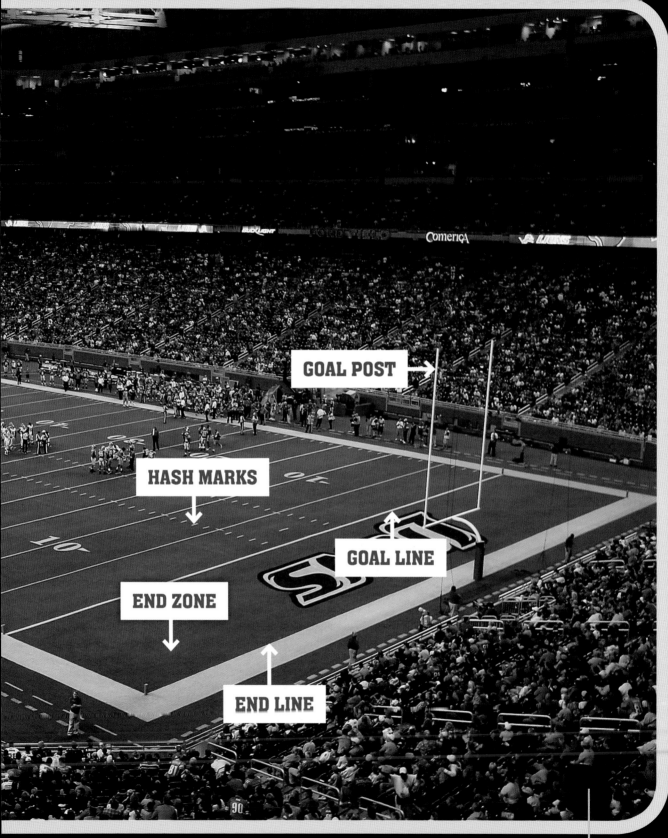

GOAL POST

HASH MARKS

GOAL LINE

END ZONE

END LINE

BIG DAYS

The Lions have had some great moments in their history. Here are three of the greatest:

1952—The Lions went 9-3 during the regular season. They had the top **defense** in the NFL. Detroit made the NFL Championship Game. The Lions met the Cleveland Browns on December 28. Detroit's defense was strong again. The Lions won 17-7 for the title.

1957—Detroit won its fourth NFL Championship. It was the team's third in six years. The Lions again beat the Cleveland Browns. This time the **offense** was on display. Detroit won 59-14 on December 29.

The Lions beat the Cleveland Browns on November 2, 1952, before beating them again for that year's NFL Championship on December 28.

1997—Running back Barry Sanders is among the best Lions players ever. This was his greatest season. He rushed for 2,053 yards. That was the second most in a single season at the time. He was named the league **Most Valuable Player (MVP)**.

TOUGH DAYS

Football is a hard game. Even the best teams have rough games and seasons. Here are some of the toughest times in Lions history:

1942—The Lions failed to win a game. They went 0-11. Detroit was terrible on offense. The Lions scored just 38 points the entire season.

1999—Barry Sanders was one of the best players in the NFL. But he suddenly decided to retire. Sanders said he lost the drive to play. He had gotten sick of losing. The Lions wanted Sanders to repay some of his **contract** money. The two sides got into an ugly argument.

Quarterback Dan Orlovsky played in ten games during Detroit's nightmare 0–16 2008 season.

2008—Detroit became the first NFL team to finish 0–16. The Lions allowed more than 32 points per game. That was the worst in the league.

MEET THE FANS

Lions fans have seen a lot of losing. But they have stayed loyal. The city of Detroit has gone through some tough times recently. Many people have lost their jobs. But they still have the Lions. The team has helped the city get through the hard period. Detroit's mascot is named Roary. He gets fans excited. When the Lions are doing well, Ford Field gets rocking.

Roary helps get Detroit fans pumped up for the Lions.

HEROES THEN

The first star in Lions history was running back Earl "Dutch" Clark. He led the NFL in rushing **touchdowns** three times. Halfback Doak Walker played for only six years. He made the Pro Bowl in five of them. Cornerback Dick LeBeau played his entire 14-year career in Detroit. He was a smart defender. He went on to coach for more than 40 years in the NFL. Barry Sanders is one of the best running backs in league history. He played from 1989 to 1998. Sanders is the only Lion to be named NFL MVP. He retired with 15,269 rushing yards. That was second in NFL history at the time. He also had 109 touchdowns in his career. If he had not retired early, he might hold many NFL rushing records.

Defensive back Dick LeBeau, one of the smartest players on the field, used his knowledge during his long and successful coaching career.

HEROES NOW

Wide receiver Calvin Johnson is nicknamed "Megatron." His size and speed make him almost impossible to cover. The Lions drafted him second overall in 2007. Johnson has led the NFL in receiving yards twice. He set an NFL record with 1,964 receiving yards in 2012. Quarterback Matthew Stafford has one of the strongest arms in the league. He had at least 4,600 passing yards every year from 2011 to 2013. Defensive end Ezekiel Ansah led the team with eight sacks as a rookie in 2013. His nickname is "Ziggy."

Quarterback Matthew Stafford has racked up the yards since entering the NFL in 2009.

GEARING UP

NFL players wear team uniforms. They wear helmets and pads to keep them safe. Cleats help them make quick moves and run fast. Some players wear extra gear for protection.

THE FOOTBALL

NFL footballs are made of leather. Under the leather is a lining that fills with air to give the ball its shape. The leather has bumps or "pebbles." These help players grip the ball. Laces help players control their throws. Footballs are also called "pigskins" because some of the first balls were made from pig bladders. Today they are made of leather from cows.

Wide receiver Calvin Johnson led the NFL in receiving yards in 2011 and 2012.

HELMET

SHOULDER PADS

GLOVES

THIGH PADS

FOOTBALL

CLEATS

SPORTS STATS

ere are some of the all-time career records for the Detroit Lions. All the stats are through the 2014 season.

PASSING YARDS

Matthew Stafford 21,714

Bobby Layne 15,710

INTERCEPTIONS

Dick LeBeau 62

Lem Barney 56

RECEPTIONS

Herman Moore 670

Calvin Johnson 643

SACKS

Robert Porcher 95.5

Mike Cofer 62.5

TOTAL TOUCHDOWNS

Barry Sanders 109

Calvin Johnson 75

POINTS

Jason Hanson 2,150

Eddie Murray 1,113

Running back Barry Sanders made the Pro Bowl in each of his ten NFL seasons, leading the league in rushing yards four times.

RUSHING YARDS

Barry Sanders 15,269

Billy Sims 5,106

GLOSSARY

contract an agreement about how much and for how long a team pays a player

defense the unit of a football team that tries to keep the other team from scoring

league an organization of sports teams that compete against each other

Most Valuable Player (MVP) a yearly award given to the top player in the NFL

offense the unit of a football team that has the ball and tries to score points

rivals teams whose games bring out the greatest emotion between the players and the fans on both sides

Super Bowl the championship game of the NFL, played between the winners of the AFC and the NFC

touchdowns plays in which the ball is held in the other team's end zone, resulting in six points

FIND OUT MORE

IN THE LIBRARY

Bodden, Valerie. *The Big Time: Calvin Johnson.*
Mankato, MN: Creative Education, 2014.

Editors of Sports Illustrated Kids. *Sports Illustrated
Kids Football: Then to WOW!* New York:
Sports Illustrated, 2014.

Frisch, Nate. *NFL Today: The Story of the Detroit Lions.*
Mankato, MN: Creative Paperbacks, 2013.

ON THE WEB

Visit our Web site for links about the Detroit Lions:
childsworld.com/links

*Note to Parents, Teachers, and Librarians: We routinely verify our Web links to make
sure they are safe and active sites. So encourage your readers to check them out!*

INDEX